I am dedicating this book to all the creatures in the ocean. It is not their fault that people litter. It is important to clean up the beach so animals don't get sick or die. For my summer vacation this year I am going to Florida and I plan to clean up the beach.

Deep in the ocean there was a beautiful underwater city. The city was called Shellville. It had many homes, a school, office buildings and a hospital.

A dolphin named Daphne lived there and played with her friends every day. Their favorite game to play was hide n seek tag.

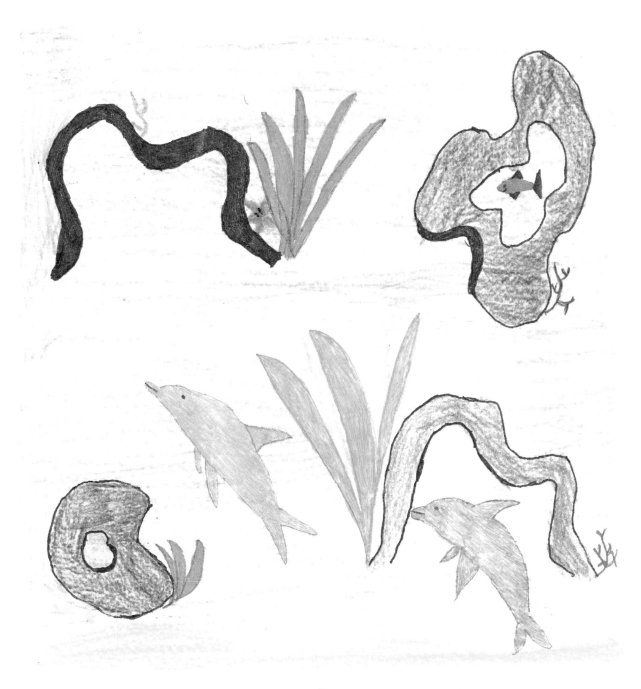

One day while they were playing, one of Daphne's friends gave her a necklace. She told Daphne it was a very special necklace and to keep it very safe, and told her that she is now old enough and ready to have the responsibility of what may come with it. Daphne was very happy and thanked her friend and promised to keep it very safe.

She kept the necklace safe at all times even when she went to bed.

In the morning Daphne swam to her friends to play. She woke up extra early that morning and was very tired. When she found her friends they said, "Go to the beach and rest, we can play games when you wake up." When Daphne got to the beach she slid onto the sand which made her necklace spark and shimmer. Daphne turned into a human!!!

Daphne felt silly. She looked and saw that she had feet! She had hands! She had a small nose! She felt very weird not being in the water. She tried to stand up and walk but she fell down on the sand. Daphne knew that she could do it. So she took a deep breath and she tried again and, she did it! She walked!! Her friends swam up to the beach looking for her but only saw a human standing there. Daphne walked down to the water to show her friends what happened. Daphne was so grateful to her friend for giving her this magical necklace, but also a little sad because she did not want to be the only one.

Daphne's friend that gave her the necklace told her that she also had a magical necklace that can turn her into a human. All of their dolphin friends do. Daphne swam around with joy because when she turned into a human on the beach, she would have a friend with her. The next day Daphne went to go get her friend. They went to the beach together. They pressed their necklaces on the sandy beach and they were both a human.

Once they turned into a human, Daphne had an idea. The idea was they would go get lots of gloves and trash bags, bring them back to the beach and pick up glass, plastic, and trash. Daphne's friend thought that was a good idea. So they went to the store to get gloves and trash bags. Once they got back to the beach there were lots of people on the beach. Once Daphne and her friend started to clean up the people on the beach wanted to help. So they started collecting trash.

Soon Daphne and her friend got on the news because of how helpful they were to the animals in the ocean and the environment. Now most of the glass, plastic and trash was cleaned up, but there were lots of beaches to go. Before Daphne and her friend did that they went back to the ocean to get some rest.

When they got done resting Daphne and her friend noticed it was 11:30 p.m. so Daphne and her friend went back to sleep. In the morning Daphne and her friend went to go say hi to their friends. They told them what happened and what a big day it had been.

They went to the store and got gloves and trash bags. And started to pick the trash up at a different beach. When Daphne and her friend got to the beach it was already clean. The people said, "We saw you on the news and we wanted to help."

After the news aired more and more people started to clean up on the beach and everywhere else they went. Even Daphne and her friend still come and help clean.

"Everyone has free time and if you work hard then you can be like Daphne and make big changes in the world.   The environment is counting on you!!"

- Mallory Blume

Mallory Blume is a young author who began writing when she was six years old. She loves to write and draw. During the summer her hobbies include boating, tubing, and swimming with her family and friends.   She is an animal lover and has experience riding a dolphin. She also loves to dance and is very involved in dance competitions.   Mallory has not yet decided what she wants to be when she grows up, but she will always be a writer.

Activity Pages

Now its your turn to be the creative one!

What would your magical magnificent necklace look like, and what powers would it have?

Write and draw below:

_____

_____

_____

_____

_____

What would you do to help the environment?

Write and draw below:

_____

_____

_____

_____

_____

N	R	S	O	R	A	E	T	T	R	L	S	E	H
L	D	A	O	D	H	M	N	R	S	A	I	N	F
U	E	A	N	C	A	D	E	M	A	E	C	V	R
R	E	S	U	E	R	O	N	I	O	S	L	I	I
O	N	U	L	O	C	A	H	E	R	C	H	R	E
A	C	K	H	V	O	O	P	C	T	N	H	O	N
N	S	E	P	O	I	L	A	E	O	A	S	N	D
A	A	A	A	N	T	N	D	L	S	E	S	M	S
L	N	L	N	N	R	E	T	T	I	L	T	E	R
P	D	N	D	P	O	L	L	U	T	I	O	N	T
S	D	H	C	A	E	B	O	E	C	H	C	T	N
N	E	C	K	L	A	C	E	P	N	S	T	N	T
O	L	E	M	H	I	H	N	I	H	P	L	O	D
N	E	S	L	N	M	A	G	I	C	A	L	R	C

DAPHNE

SAND

REUSE

ENVIRONMENT

TRASH

DOLPHIN

NECKLACE

MAGICAL

FRIENDS

POLLUTION

OCEAN

BEACH

LITTER

Write and draw about a time at the beach:

_____

_____

_____

_____

_____

If you would be any ocean animal what would it be?

Write and draw below:

_____

_____

_____

_____

_____

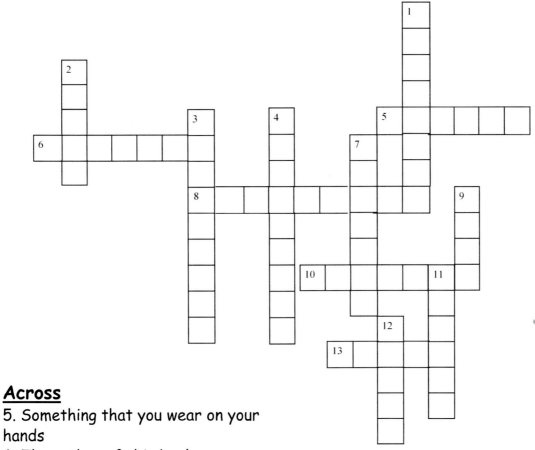

Across

5. Something that you wear on your hands
6. The author of this book
8. The city where Daphne lives
10. The close bond with two or more people

13. An area full of sand

Down

1. The magical item
2. Something that covers over 70% of the world
3. Something that you put garbage in
4. Humans are doing this to our oceans and beaches
7. Playful and intelligent ocean animal
9. Something you can read or watch to know what is going on in the world
11. Main character in book
12. The power of the necklace

Here are some ways how you can help the ocean:

- Use reusable bottles and straws
- Recycle
- Use fewer plastic products
- Spread the word
- Leave nothing behind
- Don't use plastic bags
- Conserve water
- Be involved and know what's going on

Ocean oil spill activity

What you will need:

- Large clear plastic bowl
- water
- blue food coloring
- ladle or other spoons
- ocean sea animals, boats etc.
- olive oil or baby oil
- liquid dish soap
- feather

What to do:

-Fill bowl with water (half full, so there is plenty of room to play)

-Add 2-3 drops of blue food

- Mix to make "ocean water"

- Add toys

- Add 10-15 drops of oil

-Observe the change in the water. What does it feel like? How does it look? What do your ocean toys feel like?

- Now try with spoons or any tools to remove the oil from the water.

- Dip a feather in the water and see how that changes

- Finally squirt some liquid dish soap into your water and observe what happens. Does the oil disappear?

FACT PAGE

- Oceans cover 71% of the world.

- By 2050 plastic will outweigh the ocean's fish population.

- Plastic is one of the most common pollution items in the oceans today which is especially harmful because it does not breakdown easily and is often mistaken as food by ocean animals.

- Over 1 million sea birds and 100,000 ocean mammals are killed by pollution each year.

- Dolphins are warm-blooded and have blubber to help keep them worm.

- Dolphins give birth to only one baby every 1-6 years.

- Orca (Killer Whale) is part of the dolphin family

https://www.conservation.org/stories/ocean-pollution-11-facts-you-need-to-know?gclid=Cj0KCQiAr8bwBRD4ARIsAHa4YyJ3-fZqUBqWGAke1eS_MB2q6y2JyeG0T0aJTbMj50yVObG91TkeEkMaArgAEALw_wcB

https://www.rubiconglobal.com/blog/ocean-pollution-facts/

https://www.dosomething.org/us/facts/11-facts-about-pollution

https://uk.whales.org/whales-dolphins/facts-about-dolphins/

Made in the USA
Monee, IL
26 October 2022

16561794R00017